The Lunar Chronicles

Coloring Book

A FEIWEL AND FRIENDS BOOK

An Imprint of Macmillan Publishing Group, LLC

THE LUNAR CHRONICLES COLORING BOOK. Copyright © 2016 by Rampion Books. All rights reserved.

Printed in China by RR Donnelley Asia Printing Solutions Ltd., Dongguan City, Guangdong Province.

For information, address Feiwel and Friends, 175 Fifth Avenue, New York, N.Y. 10010.

Our books may be purchased in bulk for promotional, educational, or business use.

Please contact your local bookseller or the Macmillan Corporate and Premium Sales Department

at (800) 221-7945 ext. 5442 or by e-mail at MacmillanSpecialMarkets@macmillan.com.

Library of Congress Cataloging-in-Publication Data is available.

ISBN 978-1-250-12360-2

Book design by Sophie Erb

Feiwel and Friends logo designed by Filomena Tuosto

First Edition—2016

1 3 5 7 9 10 8 6 4 2

fiercereads.com

Marissa Meyer

The Lunar Chronicles

Coloring Book

illustrated by

Kathryn Gee

Feiwel and Friends
New York

Introduction

Marissa Meyer

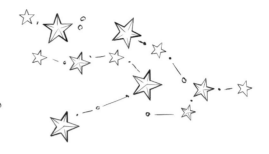

It was during my book tour for *Stars Above: A Lunar Chronicles Collection* that the idea for this coloring book began to take hold. It wasn't my idea, or even my publisher's, but rather the fans—those brilliant self-dubbed Lunartics—who started to ask me, at nearly every bookstore I visited, if a coloring book was in the works.

Just a few years earlier, this would have been an impossible fantasy. After all, regular old book series don't get coloring books! Those are reserved for children and big franchises. Thirty-two pages of princess line art or farm animal activities, sure, but my young adult space opera? I'll keep dreaming!

But then, seemingly overnight, a coloring book craze started to sweep through the book world, and coloring was no longer just for kids. As it turns out, it's a perfectly acceptable way for teenagers and adults to reduce stress, increase concentration, and explore creativity. Who knew? What's more, a trend that started out as abstract zen drawings was quickly expanding to include, of all things, beloved book series. So the impossible fantasy of a Lunar Chronicles coloring book started to seem, well, possible.

One other surprising thing happened on that *Stars Above* tour. It started at the launch party in Seattle, when a fan handed me an envelope containing a handful of 4x4 squares of paper, each with a fragment of a drawing on them. She instructed me to hold on to the squares throughout the tour as there would be more coming and, at the end, they would combine to make "one epic image." She was right—at nearly every event, someone would eventually arrive at my signing table with an envelope full of colorful puzzle pieces.

I soon began to anticipate these deliveries, becoming giddy each time a new batch was handed to me. After the events, my publicist and I would sit at a table at our hotel bar assembling the pieces, trying to interpret the newest squares (*Look, it's Winter! It's Scarlet! I . . . have no idea what that is. OMG it's Iko!*), and watching as the complete image was slowly revealed.

Most impressive to me was that one fan-artist, Kathryn Gee, had coordinated the whole endeavor. Not only had she drawn the image for the puzzle, but she had divided it into pieces and given each one to a professed Lunartic, encouraging them to color their square as they saw fit. Each of the twenty-eight contributors even wrote a heartfelt message on the back of their piece before mailing them to those who would be attending the events, in order to be delivered to me.

I was amazed by the ingenuity and organization it must have taken to pull off. And, once all the pieces were assembled and the image was revealed, I was staggered by how beautiful and, yes, *epic* it was.* Those abstract 4x4 squares had turned into a portrait of the entire Lunar Chronicles crew, thoughtfully colored by readers who had joined Cinder and her allies for every trial, adventure, and victory. It was an inspiring collaboration, and one of the most meaningful gifts I have ever received.

Not long after I returned home, I told my publisher that fans kept asking for a coloring book, and was surprised and delighted when they felt the idea had potential. I was even more delighted when they agreed to consider a wild and crazy idea—I wanted a fan-artist to do the artwork, and I already had just the artist in mind.

Though I had never met Kathryn before, it was easy to track down her artwork online, and once my publisher saw her talent and the enthusiasm she had for the Lunar Chronicles, we all felt she was exactly the right person to bring this coloring book to life. We were all so thrilled when she agreed to be a part of this project.

From the start, we wanted this book to be by a fan, for the fans. I think we've accomplished that. I love that reader support has made a Lunar Chronicles coloring book not so impossible after all, and I look forward to seeing how all you talented colorists are going interpret the world, the characters, and Kathryn's gorgeous artwork.

So sharpen those pencils, Lunartics. We have coloring to do!

* *The original artwork is included as the final illustration of this book.*

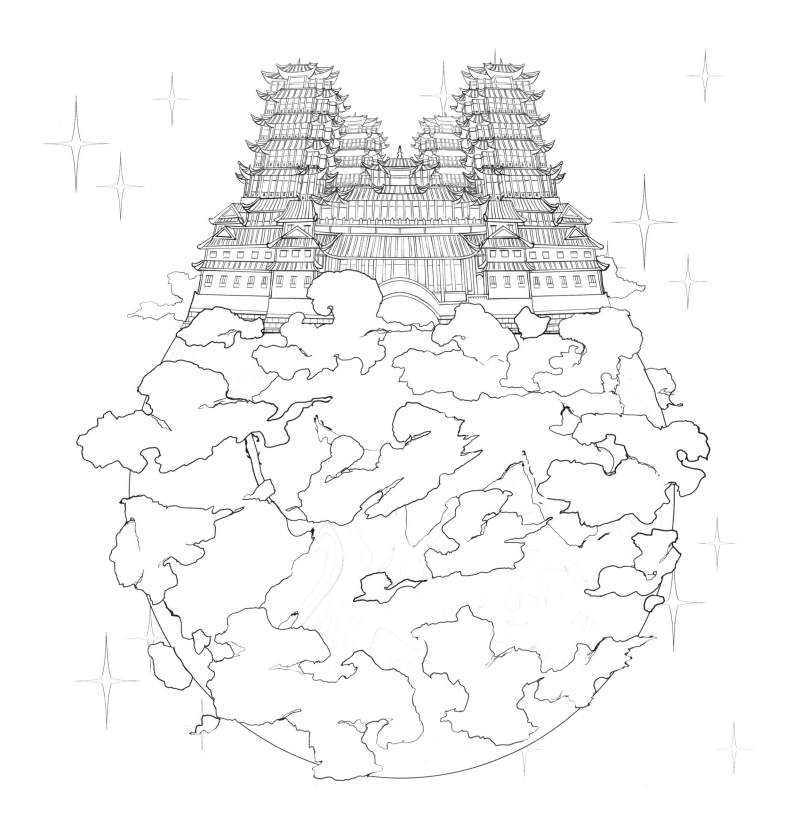

The Crew

When I first started conceptualizing the Lunar Chronicles, my hopes and plans for the series often seemed hopelessly complicated, sometimes overwhelmingly so. There was just so much going on in these books, even in my earliest dreaming of them. There were spaceships and fairy tales, robots and plagues, biogenetically engineered super-soldiers and a society of crazy mind-controlling sycophants on the moon. There were tangled backstories and intertwining subplots. There were overlapping romances and family dramas, heists and prison breaks and rebellions and everything in between. The more I allowed the story to grow in my mind—and, eventually, on paper—the more complex and intricate it became.

However, when I waded through all the action and all the adventure, I found that the tale I was really trying to tell was about the relationships that form between the main characters, and how those bonds would change and strengthen them. This was to be the story of Linh Cinder, a cyborg mechanic who was destined to change the world, but couldn't possibly do it on her own. I was eager to watch Cinder grow from an outcast to a leader, all the while gathering a ragtag group of heroes and antiheroes around her in her crusade to take down the evil queen.

It might seem like a big story, with all those wars and revolutions running amok, but it's really the tale of nine unlikely heroes who became not just allies, but friends. This is the story of Cinder and her crew.

Linh Cinder

Thorne waved his hand. "They already showed the clips. And now you've achieved the dream of every red-blooded girl under the age of twenty-five."

"Right," said Cinder. "My life is a real dream come true."

Thorne wiggled his eyebrow. "Maybe not, but at least dreamy Prince Kai knows your name."

"*Emperor* Kai," she said, frowning at him.

"Precisely." Thorne cocked his head toward the front of the ship. "They're starting a press conference, to talk about *you*. Thought you wouldn't want to miss"— Thorne fanned himself, swooning— "his heavenly, chocolate-brown eyes, and perfectly tousled hair, and—"

Cinder sprang off the bed, shoving Thorne into the doorframe as she marched past him.

"Ow," he said, rubbing his arm. "What's got your wires crossed?"

(From *Scarlet,* ch. 24)

Emperor Kaito

"I want you to know that I hold nothing against you," Iko said, by way of introduction. "I understand that it isn't your fault your programmer had so little imagination."

The escort-droid held her gaze with empty eyes.

"In another life, we could have been sisters, and I feel it's important to acknowledge that."

A blank stare. A blink, every six seconds.

"But as it stands, I'm a part of an important mission right now, and I cannot be swayed from my goal by my sympathy for androids who are less advanced than myself."

(From *Cress,* ch. 46)

Iko

"This Scarlet . . ." said Cress, "you're in love with her, aren't you?"

Wolf froze, becoming stone still. As the hover climbed the hill to the palace his shoulders sank, and he returned his gaze to the window. "She's my alpha," he murmured, with a haunting sadness in his voice.

Alpha.

Cress leaned forward, propping her elbows on her knees. "Like the star?"

"What star?"

She stiffened, instantly embarrassed, and scooted back from him again. "Oh. Um. In a constellation, the brightest star is called the alpha. I thought maybe you meant that she's . . . like . . . your brightest star." Looking away, she knotted her hands in her lap, aware that she was blushing furiously now and this beast of a man was about to realize what an over-romantic sap she was.

But instead of sneering or laughing, Wolf sighed. "Yes," he said, his gaze climbing up to the full moon that had emerged over the city. "Exactly like that."

(From *Cress,* ch. 47)

Scarlet Benoit

"You should head to Toulouse, or even Paris," said Scarlet. "There are more jobs in the cities, and people around here don't take too kindly to strangers, as you may have noticed."

Wolf tilted his head so that his emerald eyes glowed even brighter in the wash of the ship's floodlights, looking almost amused. "Thanks for the tip."

Turning, Scarlet sank into the pilot's seat.

Wolf shifted toward the wall as she started the engine. "If you change your mind about needing a hand, I can be found at the abandoned Morel house most nights. I may not be great with people, but I think I'd do well on a farm." Amusement touched the corners of his lips. "Animals love me."

"Oh, I'm sure they do," Scarlet said, beaming with fake encouragement. She shut the door before muttering, "What farm animals don't love a wolf?"

(From *Scarlet,* ch. 3)

Ze'ev "Wolf" Kesley

All Cress could see were the blue eyes staring back at her, *directly* back at her, beginning to fill with the same breathless awe she felt.

The same wonder.

The same enchantment.

Though they were separated by two screens and vast amounts of empty space, she could feel the link being forged between them in that look. A bond that couldn't be broken. Their eyes had met for the first time, and by the look of pure amazement on his face, she knew he felt it too.

Heat crept up into her cheeks. Her hands began to shake.

"Aces," Carswell Thorne murmured. Dropping his feet to the ground, he leaned forward to inspect her closer. "Is that all *hair?*"

(From *Cress*, ch. 5)

Crescent Moon "Cress" Darnel

"Who's the other fugitive?" Kai asked, stalling for time while he struggled to grasp the implications. Cinder—a Lunar, a cyborg, a fugitive, who he'd all but sentenced to death.

Escaped.

"Carswell Thorne," said Huy, "an ex-cadet for the American Republic Air Force. He deserted his post fourteen months ago after stealing a military cargoship. At this time we don't consider him dangerous."

Kai neared his desk again, seeing that the fugitive's profile had been transferred to the screen. His frown deepened. Perhaps not dangerous, but young and inarguably good-looking. His prison photo showed him flippantly winking at the camera. Kai hated him immediately.

(From *Scarlet,* ch. 7)

Captain Carswell Thorne

"*Stars,*" whispered Iko. "You're beautiful."

A loud click echoed through the alley. "Drop your glamour," demanded Thorne, aiming a gun at the princess.

Scarlet's pulse hiccupped. "Wait—" she started, but Cinder had already put a hand on his wrist and was pressing the gun back down.

"It's not a glamour," she said.

"*Really?*" Thorne leaned toward Cinder and whispered, "Are you *sure?*"

"I'm sure."

This statement was followed by another long, heady silence, during which Winter passed her sweetest smile between each of them.

Thorne clicked the safety on and shoved the gun back into its holster. "Holy spades, you Lunars have good genes." An awkward pause followed, before he added, "Who is she?"

"This is Winter," said Scarlet. "Princess Winter."

(From *Winter,* ch. 32)

Princess Winter Hayle-Blackburn

Jacin raised his head as she reached the edge of the dais. Their eyes clashed, and she was staring at a man who had been beaten and bound and mocked and tormented all day and for a moment Winter was sure he was broken. Another one of the queen's broken toys.

But then one side of his mouth lifted, and the smile hit his startling blue eyes, and he was as bright and welcoming as the rising sun.

"Hey, Trouble," he said, leaning his head back against the dial.

With that, the terror from the past weeks slipped away. He was alive. He was home. He was still Jacin.

(From *Winter,* ch. 3)

Sir Jacin Clay

Allies & Villains

A story cannot revolve around its heroes alone. There must be a counterpart, an opposition, and in the Lunar Chronicles, wicked Queen Levana was more than happy to fill that role. Of course, like most villains, she would never admit to being the bad guy. She had her own dreams and ambitions—and who was that pesky cyborg mechanic to try to take it all away from her, anyway? Levana's story grew simultaneously beside Cinder's—ever expanding and changing until their paths were so tightly knotted together that their fates became inseparable. As I learned more and more about Levana, her past and her secrets and the truth she kept hidden beneath her glamour (for years, a truth she kept hidden even from me!), I became fascinated by her story. From the start, Queen Levana was one of my favorite characters to uncover.

And then there are those "minor" characters who are constantly catching me off guard (and would no doubt hate being called *minor* at all). It's not uncommon for a character to arrive on the scene as someone who is there merely to move the plot along and then get out of the way so the heroes can take over. But it's also not uncommon for some of those secondary characters to develop stories of their own, and sometimes I can't help but find myself falling in love with them . . . or loathing them, as the case might be. Secondary characters can be blatant show-stealers, and they often add a richness to the story in ways I never would have expected.

Cinder and the crew meet a lot of people in the course of their travels—some who offer help, protection, and guidance, and others who do everything in their power to throw them off course.

Here are some of my show-stealers.

Queen Levana

"Tell me," Sybil demanded. "*Speculate* if you must. Where would she have gone?"

"I have no idea."

Scarlet's other hand slammed onto the top of the block, fingers splayed out against the dark wood. She gasped at her own sudden movements, finally tearing her gaze away from the queen to stare at her traitorous limb.

"Perhaps an easier question, then."

Scarlet jumped. Sybil was right behind her now, whispering against her ear.

"Which finger do you value the least?"

(From *Cress,* ch. 42)

"We are perfectly matched," said Aimery. "You are beautiful and adored. I am powerful and respected. You are in need of a partner who can protect you with his gift to offset your own disabilities. Think of it. The princess and the queen's head thaumaturge—we will be the greatest envy of the court."

His eyes were shining and it became clear he had been imagining this for a long time. Winter had often thought Aimery might be attracted to her, and this knowledge had been the seed for countless nightmares. She *knew* how he treated the women he was attracted to.

(From *Winter,* ch. 18)

Thaumaturges Sybil Mira and Aimery Park

There were *people*.

Not many, but a dozen at least, mingling around one of the larger ships. They were too far to see clearly, but Cress could make out vibrant-colored clothing, and one of the men was wearing an enormous hat and—

Sybil grabbed Cress's elbow and yanked her in the opposite direction. Cress gasped and stumbled after her.

"Do not look at them," said Sybil.

Cress frowned. Her arm was stinging but she resisted the urge to rip it out of Sybil's grip. "Why? Who are they?"

"They are members of Artemisia's families, and they would not appreciate being gawked at by a *shell*."

(From "After Sunshine Passes By," *Stars Above*)

A Lunar aristocrat

Squinting, Cinder jutted a finger at the doctor. "You *did* use your mind control on me. When we met. You . . . you brainwashed me. Just like the queen. You made me trust you."

"Be fair. You were attacking me with a wrench."

Her anger wavered.

Dr. Erland opened his palms to her. "I assure you, Miss Linh, in the twelve years that I have been on Earth, I have not abused the gift once, and I am paying the price for that decision every day. My mental stability, my psychological health, my very senses are failing me because I refuse to manipulate the thoughts and feelings of those around me. Not all Lunars can be trusted—I know that as well as anyone—but you *can* trust me."

(From *Cinder*, ch. 25)

Dr. Dmitri Erland

She might have pointed out that Pearl and Peony could have been given ready-made rather than custom dresses in order to budget for Cinder's as well. She might have pointed out that they would only wear their dresses one time too. She might have pointed out that, as she was the one doing the work, the money should have been hers to spend as she saw fit. But all arguments would come to nothing. Legally, Cinder belonged to Adri as much as the household android and so too did her money, her few possessions, even the new foot she'd just attached. Adri loved to remind her of that.

So she stomped the anger down before Adri could see a spark of rebellion.

(From *Cinder,* ch. 2)

Linh Adri and her daughters, Pearl and Peony

The World of
The Lunar Chronicles

Creating the world of the Lunar Chronicles was a gradual process. It was constantly expanding and changing as I wrote, the plots of each book revealing new secrets the world had to offer— and oftentimes, those secrets turning around to influence the plot as well. Early on, I wanted the series to have a global feel. I hoped the reader would sense that while these characters start their journeys separated by continents, oceans, and space, they were still connected to each other and to the rest of humanity. The wars, plagues, and injustices they faced were problems that affected every Earthen and Lunar. This is in part why I embraced such a variety of settings in the story— from the metropolis of New Beijing to rural Rieux, France. From the sandy Sahara Desert to the terra-formed biodomes of Luna.

From there, I chose specific settings as a way to pay homage to the tales that inspired the story. Futuristic China was selected because a ninth-century Chinese fairy tale titled "Ye Xian" is believed by many to be the first recorded version of what would later become "Cinderella." *Scarlet* is set in France because of the country's ties to werewolf mythology, particularly the "Beast of Gévaudan" mystery, in which two hundred brutal murders in the 1700s were suspected to be the result of a rampaging werewolf. For *Cress*, I was drawn to a line in "Rapunzel" in which (depending on the version you're reading) the witch casts Rapunzel out into "a great desert." And when I think of a great desert, I can't help but think of the Sahara.

Then there was my favorite setting to explore—Luna. From the dusty, impoverished outer sectors to the glittering, frivolous white city of Artemisia, my imagination had only the bounds of science to contend with, and even then I tried not to let it hold me back.

Over time, the challenge of bringing these landscapes to life in ways that were authentic and integral to the story became one of the most rewarding parts of writing the Lunar Chronicles.

Artemisia Palace

Towering offices and shopping centers gradually melded with a messy assortment of apartment buildings, built so close that they became an unending stretch of glass and concrete. Apartments in this corner of the city had once been spacious and desirable but had been so subdivided and remodeled over time—always trying to cram more people into the same square footage—that the buildings had become labyrinths of corridors and stairwells.

But all the crowded ugliness was briefly forgotten as Cinder turned the corner onto her own street. For half a step, New Beijing Palace could be glimpsed between complexes, sprawling and serene on the cliff that overlooked the city. The palace's pointed gold roofs sparkled orange beneath the sun, the windows glinting the light back at the city. The ornate gables, the tiered pavilions that teetered dangerously close to the cliff's edge, the rounded temples stretching to the heavens.

(From *Cinder,* ch. 2)

 New Beijing

"If you had even one small thing that brought you happiness, or hope that things could someday be better, then maybe that would be enough to sustain you. Otherwise, I fear it will be too easy for the queen to win."

"And what would you suggest?"

Priya shrugged. "Perhaps this garden is a good place to start?"

Following her gesture, Kai took in the stalks of bamboo bowing over the stone walls, the myriad lilies beginning to fade after summer's long showing, the bright fish that clustered and pressed against each other, ignorant of the turmoil in the world above their small pond.

It was beautiful.

(From *Cress,* ch. 19)

In the gardens of New Beijing Palace

The sun was sinking fast, sending Scarlet's elongated shadow down the drive. Beyond the gravel, the whispering crops of cornstalks and leafy sugar beets stretched out in every direction, meeting up with the first spray of stars. A cobblestone house disrupted the view to the west, with two windows glowing orange. Their only neighbor for miles.

For more than half her life, this farm had been Scarlet's paradise. Over the years, she'd fallen in love with it more deeply than she'd known a person could fall in love with land and sky—and she knew her grandma felt the same. Though she didn't like to think of it, she was aware that someday she would inherit the farm, and she sometimes fantasized about growing old here. Happy and content, with perpetual dirt beneath her fingernails and an old house that was in constant need of repair.

(From *Scarlet*, ch. 5)

Benoit Farms and Gardens

Her satellite made one full orbit around planet Earth every sixteen hours. It was a prison that came with an endlessly breathtaking view—vast blue oceans and swirling clouds and sunrises that set half the world on fire.

When she was first imprisoned, she had loved nothing more than to stack her pillows on top of the desk that had been built into the walls and drape her bed linens over the screens, making a small alcove for herself. She would pretend that she was not on a satellite at all, but in a podship en route to the blue planet. Soon she would land and step out onto real dirt, feel real sunshine, smell real oxygen.

She would stare at the continents for hours and hours, imagining what that must be like.

(From *Cress,* ch. 1)

Cress's satellite

"It's beautiful out there."

A hesitation, before, "Could you be more specific?"

"The sky is this gorgeous, intense blue color." She pressed her fingers to the glass and traced the wavy hills on the horizon.

"Oh good. You've really narrowed it down for me."

"I'm sorry, it's just . . ." She tried to stamp down the rush of emotion. "I think we're in a desert."

"Cactuses and tumbleweeds?"

"No. Just a lot of sand. It's kind of orangeish-gold, with hints of pink, and I can see tiny clouds of it floating above the ground, like . . . like smoke."

"Piled up in lots of hills?"

"Yes, exactly! And it's *beautiful*."

Thorne snorted. "If this is how you feel about a desert, I can't wait until you see your first real tree. Your mind will explode."

(From *Cress*, ch. 15)

The Sahara Desert

Winter's heart fluttered as she pushed open the massive glass door to the menagerie. Sounds of wildlife spilled into the corridor—squawking birds in their palatial cages, monkeys chattering from overhead vines, white stallions neighing in distant stables.

She shut the door before the heat could escape and scanned the forked pathways, but there was no sign of Jacin. The menagerie took up several acres of this wing of the palace, a labyrinth of barred cages and glass enclosures. It was always humid and perfumed with exotic flowers, an aroma that barely covered up the animal scent . . .

She tucked an unruly curl behind her ear and moved away from the door. She passed the chilled home of the arctic fox, who was curled atop a birch log, hiding his face behind a bristled tail. The next cage held a mother snow leopard and her litter of three prancing cubs. On the opposite side of the mossy path was a sleeping white owl. It peeped its huge eyes open as Winter passed.

(From *Winter,* ch. 28)

The menagerie

Moments

When I'm writing, I often feel as though I'm watching a movie playing out in my imagination. My fingers race across the keyboard, trying to record what I'm seeing as fast as I can, before the moment gets away. Many of my favorite scenes from the Lunar Chronicles are those that I could envision the most clearly—so vivid that at times I felt I was living them myself. I was in that ballroom, watching Cinder descend the steps in her soaking, filthy ball gown. My pulse was racing as Scarlet slipped on the roof of the speeding maglev train. My heart was breaking as Jacin risked everything to protect Winter from her murderous stepmother.

Though these scenes can be so clear in my mind, they are often the most difficult to write, as I want them to be *perfect*. My goal is for readers to experience these moments as intensely as I do, to feel as though they are there. These become the scenes that I revise again and again, trying to capture them perfectly on the page. Sometimes this can be endlessly frustrating, as I continually rework every sentence, every word, every *comma*, hoping to land on the precise combination that will bring the scene to life.

But once the writing is finished and those frustrations are forgotten, these inevitably become my favorite scenes. These are the moments I continue to return to, on the page and in my imagination, and seeing them depicted in the artwork that follows has brought me enormous amounts of joy. These illustrations might be black-and-white as I'm writing this, but I know they won't stay that way for long.

Prince Kai at the market

The hot air caught in Kai's throat, choking him. The queen paused just long enough to seem as though she were letting her eyes adjust to the bright daylight of Earth—but Kai suspected she really just wanted him to see her.

She was indeed beautiful, as if someone had taken the scientific measurements of perfection and used them to mold a single ideal specimen. Her face was slightly heart-shaped, with high cheekbones barely flushed. Auburn hair fell in silken ringlets to her waist and her unblemished ivory skin shimmered like mother-of-pearl in the sunshine. Her lips were red red red, looking like she'd just drunk a pint of blood.

A chill shook Kai from the inside out. She was unnatural.

(From *Cinder*, ch. 20)

Queen Levana arrives on Earth

"It's from the palace. It might help. Do you understand?" Cinder kept her voice low, worried that the other patients might hear, might riot against her. But Peony's gaze remained empty. "A *cure,* Peony," she hissed against her ear. "An antidote."

Peony said nothing, head drooped against Cinder's shoulder. Her body had gone limp but she was light as a wooden doll.

Cinder's throat felt coated in sand as she stared into Peony's empty eyes. Eyes looking past her, through her.

"No . . . Peony, didn't you hear me?" Cinder pulled Peony fully against her and uncorked the vial. "You have to drink this." She held the vial to Peony's lips, but Peony didn't move. Didn't flinch. "*Peony.*"

(From *Cinder,* ch. 27)

In the letumosis quarantine

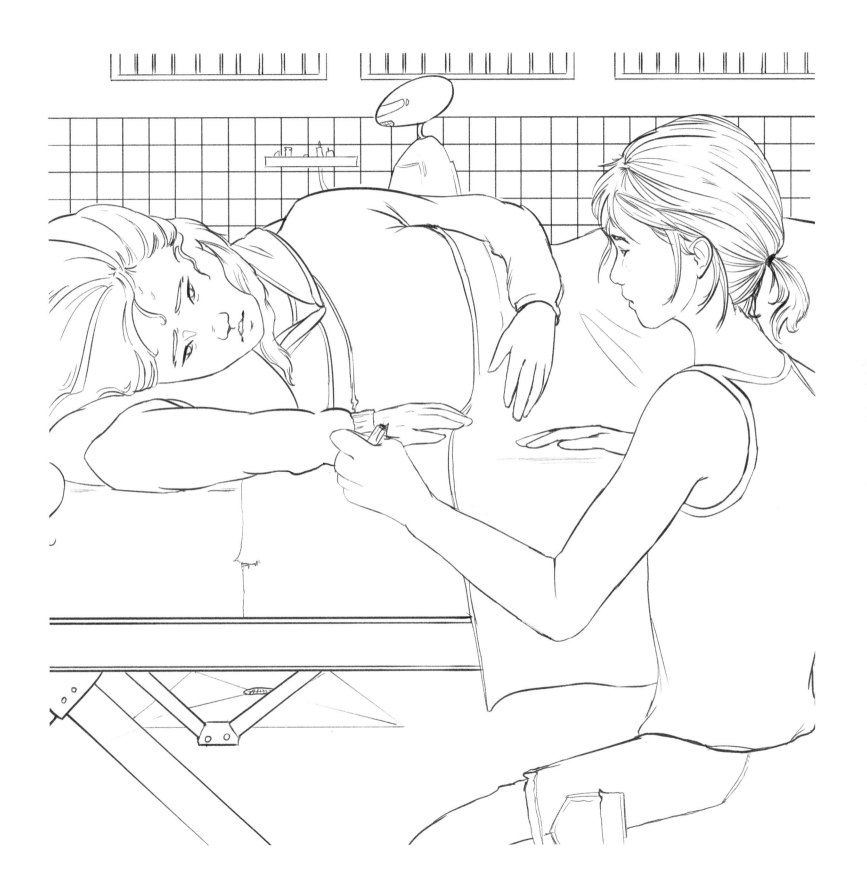

They were the only ones dancing.

Kai must have noticed it too, for he floated his hand briefly away from her waist, gesturing to the gawking crowd, and said in a tone that was part encouragement, part command, "Please, you are my guests. Enjoy the music."

Awkwardly, those nearby traded glances with their own partners, and soon the floor was filling with bustled skirts and coattails. Cinder risked glancing toward where they had abandoned Adri and Pearl—they were both standing still amid the shuffling crowd, watching as Kai expertly guided Cinder farther and farther away from them.

Clearing his throat, Kai murmured, "You have no idea how to dance, do you?"

Cinder fixed her gaze on him, mind still reeling. "I'm a *mechanic*."

His eyebrows raised mockingly. "Believe me, I noticed. Are those grease stains on the gloves I gave you?"

(From *Cinder*, ch. 34)

The 126th Annual Peace Ball

Cinder dropped the gun and ran. Knowing the frenzied crowd was impenetrable, she barreled toward the nearest exit, the massive doors that led into the gardens. Past the guard, past the queen, past her entourage, glass crunching beneath her stolen boots.

The hollow echo of the stone patio. A puddle splashing onto her legs. The fresh, cool smell of rain that had turned to a drizzle.

The stairway stretched before her. Twelve steps and a Zen garden, a towering wall, a gate, the city—escape.

On the fifth step, she heard the bolts snap. The wires tore loose, like tendons stretched to the max. She felt the loss of power at the base of her calf, sending a blind warning signal up to her brain.

(From *Cinder,* ch. 36)

Cinder fleeing from the ball

Hunter attacked with renewed vigor. Wolf took a punch in the stomach and crumpled over with a grunt. It was followed by a blow that sent him careening to the edge of the stage. He stumbled to one knee, but was up on his feet before Hunter could come closer.

He shook his head in an oddly doglike manner, wild hair flying, and then crouched with his big hands poised at his sides, staring at Hunter with that peculiar grin.

Scarlet wrapped her fingers around her sweatshirt's zipper, wondering if that tic was how Wolf had gotten his nickname.

(From *Scarlet*, ch. 8)

The fights at the abandoned Morel Farm

Wolf hadn't moved by the time she'd thrown open the front door. The chickens were already growing familiar with the stranger, pecking around his feet in search of falling seed.

Scarlet settled the gun in her arms and released the safety.

If he was surprised, he didn't show it.

"What do you want?" she yelled, startling the hens away from him. The light from the house spilled around her onto the gravel. Her shadow shifted across the drive, almost brushing Wolf's feet.

The madness from the fight was gone, and the bruises on his face were nearly invisible. He seemed calm and unconcerned with the gun, though he didn't move toward her.

After a long silence, he raised both hands to either side of his head, open palmed. "I'm sorry. I've frightened you again."

(From *Scarlet*, ch. 11)

Wolf comes to the farm

They landed heavily on the glass-smooth roof, the levitating train barely dipping from the impact, and Scarlet felt it instantly. The wrongness. Wolf slipped, his shoulders tilting too heavy to the left, his balance rocking beneath her weight.

Scarlet cried out, the momentum of the jump sending her spinning away from him toward the ledge. She dug her fingernails into his shoulders but his shirt ripped out from beneath her and then she was falling, the world tumbling around her.

(From *Scarlet,* ch. 23)

On the maglev train

Gulping, Scarlet pulled away. Her grandma's fingers clenched in a brief effort to restrict her, but then let go.

Scarlet staggered out of her seat and backed against the rail, staring at her grandmother. The familiar unkempt hair in its always crooked braid. The familiar eyes, growing colder as they peered up at her. Growing wider.

She blinked rapidly against the hallucination, and her grandmother's hands grew larger.

Repulsion ripped through Scarlet. She gripped the railing to hold herself steady.

"Who are you?"

(From *Scarlet,* ch. 29)

Thorne crept toward the tank. It was empty, but the vague imprint of a child could be seen in the goo-like lining beneath the glass dome. "What's this?"

Cinder went to fidget with her glove before remembering that it wasn't there.

"A suspended animation tank," she said, whispering as if the ghosts of unknown surgeons could be listening. "Designed to keep someone alive, but unconscious, for long periods of time."

"Aren't those illegal? Overpopulation laws or something?"

Cinder nodded. Nearing the tank, she pressed her fingers to the glass and tried to remember waking up here, but she couldn't. Only addled memories of the hangar and the farm came back to her—nothing about this dungeon. She hadn't been fully conscious until she'd been en route to New Beijing, ready to start her new life as a scared, confused orphan, and a cyborg.

(From Scarlet, ch. 31)

The secret under the farm

"Come on," said the man from behind her, stooping and hooking his elbow beneath Scarlet's armpit. "Time to go."

"No! I'm not leaving him!" She scrambled out of his hold and crawled toward Wolf's unconscious body, tying her arms around his head. The strangers gawked at her like she was mad. "He's not like the rest."

"He's exactly like the rest!" said the man. "He was trying to eat you!"

"He saved my life!"

The strangers exchanged disbelieving glances, and the girl gave a baffled shrug.

"Fine," the man said. "You take the helm."

He pulled Scarlet off Wolf while the girl grabbed Wolf's wrist and hoisted him up over her shoulder, grunting with the effort.

The man skirted behind and grabbed Wolf's legs. "Holy spades," he muttered, already breathless. "What are these guys made of?"

(From *Scarlet,* ch. 41)

The first attack

She bit her lip, withholding a reminder of all she'd done for Her Majesty during her imprisonment. Designing countless spy systems for keeping watch on Earth's leaders, hacking the communication links between diplomats, and jamming satellite signals to allow the queen's soldiers to invade Earth undetected, so that now the blood of sixteen thousand Earthens was on her hands. It made no difference. Sybil cared only about Cress's failures, and not finding Linh Cinder was Cress's biggest failure to date.

"I'm sorry, Mistress. I'll try harder."

(From *Cress,* ch. 1)

Receiving orders from Mistress Sybil

Wolf pushed himself off the crate, hurtling toward her. Cinder braced herself against the instinctive panic. The anticipation of one more hit tightened every muscle, despite the fact that he was still going easy on her.

She squeezed her eyes shut moments before impact and *focused.*

Pain shot through her head like a chisel into her brain. She gritted her teeth against it, attempting to numb herself to the waves of nausea that followed.

The impact didn't come.

"Stop. Closing. Your. Eyes."

(From *Cress,* ch. 2)

Training on the Rampion

Thorne reached behind her with his other hand and gathered a fistful of her hair. The touch sent a delicious tingle down her spine.

"Sorry, but it grows back," he said, not sounding at all apologetic. He began sawing through the tangles, one handful at a time. Grab, cut, release. Cress held perfectly still. Not because she was afraid of being cut—the knife was steady in his hand, despite the blindness, and Thorne kept the blade angled carefully away from her neck. But because it was Thorne. It was *Captain Carswell Thorne,* running his hands through her hair, his rough jaw mere inches away from her lips, his brow furrowed in concentration.

By the time he was brushing feather-soft fingers along her neck, checking for any strands he'd missed, she was dizzy with euphoria.

(From *Cress,* ch. 13)

Cress's first haircut

From the corner of her eye, Cinder saw his fingers twitch, but she didn't know whether Wolf was acknowledging that there was still hope out there, or whether he was just ticked at her for using him like this. Turning him into a puppet, just like the thaumaturge that had turned him into a monster.

Standing on the hotel step, with sixty guns trained on her, Cinder realized she was no better than that thaumaturge. This really was war, and she really was in the middle of it.

If she had to make sacrifices, she would.

(From *Cress,* ch. 41)

Surrounded in Farafrah

She was a famous net-drama actress making a big debut, and Wolf was her bodyguard. He wouldn't let anything happen to her. She simply had to hold her head high and be brave and be graceful and be confident. Her fine ball gown became a costume. The media became her adoring fans. Her spine straightened, millimeter by trembling millimeter, as the tingling darkness began to recede from her vision.

"All right?" Wolf murmured.

"I am a famous actress," she whispered back.

(From *Cress,* ch. 47)

Infiltrating the royal wedding

Winter's lip quivered, but she refused to cry. She wouldn't do that to him.

Jacin's fingers curled around his knife.

It *was* torture. Jacin looked more afraid than when he'd stood on trial. More pained now than when his torso had been stripped raw from the lashings.

This was the last time she would ever see him.

This was her last moment. Her last breath.

Suddenly, all of the politics and all of the games stopped mattering. Suddenly, she felt daring.

"Jacin," she said, with a shaky smile. "You must know. I cannot remember a time when I didn't love you. I don't think such a time ever existed."

His eyes filled with a thousand emotions. But before he could say whatever he would say, before he could kill her, Winter grabbed the front of his shirt with both hands and kissed him.

(From *Winter*, ch. 28)

By order of the queen

"I will now knot the two ribbons together," said Prime Minister Kamin, in her measured, serene voice. She had not faltered once during the ceremony. "This is to symbolize the unity of the bride and groom and also of Luna and the Eastern Commonwealth, which represents the planet of Earth on this, the eighth day of November in the 126th year of the third era." She took the ends of each ribbon between her fingers.

Kai watched with detached interest as her dark, slender fingers knotted the two ribbons together. She yanked on the ends, tightening the knot. Kai stared at it, feeling the disconnect in his mind.

He was not here.

This was not happening.

His hateful gaze betrayed him, flickering toward Levana's face. It was the briefest of looks, but she somehow managed to catch it. She smiled, and icicles stabbed at his spine.

This *was* happening. This was his bride.

(From *Winter*, ch. 47)

What had her sentence been? *Death by dismemberment.*

Cinder lowered the gun, pivoted, and ran. Past the puppet Lunars in their glittering clothes. Past the mindless servants and the dead thaumaturges and the splatters of blood and the fallen chairs and Pearl and Adri cowering in a corner. She sprinted toward the only escape—the wide-open balcony hanging above the water.

The pain in her shoulder throbbed and she used the reminder to run faster, her feet pounding against the hard marble.

She heard gunshots, but she had already jumped. The black sky opened up before her and she fell.

(From *Winter*, ch. 51)

Cinder's trial

"Is something wrong, my dear child?"

"No. No," said Winter. "For a moment you reminded me of someone. But my eyes play tricks on me sometimes. They're not very reliable."

"Oh, sweet, stupid child." The kink in the woman's back began to straighten. "We are Lunars. Our eyes are never reliable."

Winter shriveled back. The basket slipped from her hold, crashing to the ground.

Before her, Levana shed the guise of the old woman, a snake shedding its skin.

(From *Winter,* ch. 62)

The queen's deception

Jacin swiped his arm across the top, scattering the flowers. Beneath the glass, Winter looked like she was sleeping, except the preservation liquid gave her skin a bluish tinge, making her appear sickly and drawing attention to the scars on her face . . .

Despite everything, she still looked like perfection, at least to him. Her curly hair was buoyant in the tank's gel and her full lips were turned upward. It was like she was going to open her eyes and smile at him, any minute now. That teasing, taunting, irresistible smile.

(From *Winter,* ch. 73)

Beneath the glass

Kai and Winter stood at the altar encased in the light of glowing orbs, Winter holding the queen's crown and Kai a ceremonial scepter. Together, they represented how both Earth and Luna would accept her right to rule. The rest of her friends were in their reserved seats in the front row. Thorne, on the aisle, held out his hand as Cinder passed. She snorted and accepted the high five before floating up the stairs.

Winter winked at her. "Well done, Cinder-friend. You didn't trip. The hard part is over."

Kai gave a smile meant for only Cinder, even though the entire universe was watching. "She's right, that really is the hard part."

"Thank the stars," Cinder whispered back. "Now let's get this over with."

Taking in a long, shaky breath, she turned to face her kingdom.

(From *Winter,* ch. 97)

The coronation

And they all lived happily to the end of their days.

Marissa Meyer is the #1 *New York Times*–bestselling author of the Lunar Chronicles series and *Heartless*. She has been dreaming up stories since she first learned to talk, and that love of storytelling was nurtured throughout her teen years as she wrote gobs and gobs of Sailor Moon fan fiction. She has a BA in creative writing from Pacific Lutheran University and an MS in publishing from Pace University. She lives in Tacoma, Washington, with her charming husband and their delightfully mischievous twin daughters. Visit her at marissameyer.com.

Kathryn Gee is currently a college student studying business marketing and has lived in Oregon for her entire life. In addition to being a Lunartic, her interests include reading books, art, and architecture. Kathryn loves all art forms and the stories they tell and enjoys exploring them through drawing and painting. This is her first book. KathrynGee.com